DATE DUE

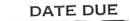

PIGEON FLIGHT

PIGEON
FLIGHT

by Mary Stolz

Pictures by Murray Tinkelman

HARPER & ROW, PUBLISHERS
New York and Evanston

For T. C. J.

PIGEON FLIGHT

On a ledge of the Plaza Hotel sat Mr. Pigeon, staring across Central Park with a black, baffled, beady eye. Some longing he did not understand stirred in his pearly-feathered breast. He paid no heed to Mrs. Pigeon, who was beside herself trying to get his attention. She strutted in a little circle on the ledge, cooing complaints in her husband's ear. But he sagged and stared as if she were not there at all.

At length, to teach him a lesson, she flew away, flut-

tering and dropping through the air to land at the Pulitzer Fountain, where she had a drink and a bath. Happily she preened and flipped her wings, tossing winks of water through the bright air. Then she hopped onto the rim to dry, smoothing each feather into place.

"We haven't seen much of your husband lately," said a voice like a bubble beside her.

Mrs. Pigeon thought of not answering. Mr. Pigeon's recent habit of hanging around the ledge, refusing to

go anywhere with her, was most upsetting. She did not
feel up to discussing it. Still—she looked closely at her
questioner—yes, it was a cousin of hers. With a cousin
one could talk over problems of a family nature.

"Ever since he retired from the William Tecumseh
Sherman monument, he's been like this," she said. "I
guess he feels there's no purpose any more."

"Nothing to keep him from patrolling General Sherman," said the cousin. "We're free as birds and can
patrol where we wish. I fancy the right front leg, myself."

Mrs. Pigeon said sadly, "When you've had the General's head for such a long time, patrolling the horse's
leg is a comedown. Mr. Pigeon is very proud. He just
hates a comedown."

"It's only a comedown if he looks at it that way,"
said the cousin stoutly.

"But that's the way he does look at it."

"In that case, why did he retire?"

"Between you and me," said Mrs. Pigeon, looking
around, making sure she'd not be overheard, "it was

less a case of retiring than of being retired, if you get my meaning. He was all but pushed off the General's head by that speckled rowdy from Sixty-second Street."

"Tch, tch," said the cousin, her throat swelling in a croomb of sympathy. "That's the way it is. Always a new crowd coming up."

Mrs. Pigeon leaned over to take a reviving sip of water, and when she looked back, her cousin was gone. That, too, was the way it was. Since Mr. Pigeon was no longer high in the world of statuary, friends and relations were falling away like molting feathers.

Now she began to worry about him, alone up there on the ledge, worried about her, no doubt, wondering where she had gone who always stayed so close to his side. Would he—oh, horrors—think that she, like the others, had deserted him?

In a flurry of anxiety, she beat her way upward, back to the home ledge, back to Mr. Pigeon.

"Oh, deary me," she said, shooting her piston head back and forth across his slumped form, "have you been terribly worried?"

"About what?" he said grumpily.

"I didn't realize I'd stayed away so long."

"Have you been away?" he said. "I thought you'd just stopped talking."

"What are we going to do now?" Mrs. Pigeon asked, really quite put out. "Have you had so much as a peanut in the past two days?"

"I'm not hungry."

"But I am."

"Go and eat, then."

"I will not stir from this ledge until you do, Mr. Pigeon. I must look out for your health."

Mr. Pigeon knew there was no point in arguing when Mrs. Pigeon was looking out for his health.

"All right," he said. "We'll go down. But don't ask me to talk to any of those—those turn-tails who bobbed and bowed to me when I had the General's head and now won't give me sidewalk room."

"No, no," she assured him. "We'll keep ourselves to ourselves. We'll find some nice old man with bread crusts, or a little boy with a bag of popcorn—"

"I want peanuts," he interrupted crossly.

Mrs. Pigeon sighed. He really was in a terrible

mood. "Very well, then . . . peanuts." It was best to humor him. He had had, after all, a bad blow to his pride. Mrs. Pigeon, who did not suffer from all that pride, felt it must be a burden. "Peanuts," she repeated soothingly. "And after that we'll fly over to the Mall. You sit on Schiller and think, and I'll sit on Victor Herbert and hum."

It was a sorrow to Mrs. Pigeon that she couldn't sing, although Mr. Pigeon had pointed out to her that canaries, for their songs, lived out their lives in cages.

"It isn't," Mrs. Pigeon had explained, "so much canaries that I have in mind. To my way of thinking, they're overtrained. No, it's song sparrows and thrushes and that ilk that I envy. They sing so beautifully. And all we can do is croomb."

"Croomb's good enough for me," said Mr. Pigeon, as if that settled the matter. He was a downright bird.

They departed, now, their ledge on the Plaza and flew across the park to the chess arena, where they found several gentlemen sitting in the sun, engaged in moving their knights and bishops and pawns across stone chessboards. There were many interested on-lookers, some of whom had bags of crusts or peanuts which they distributed among the squirrels and pigeons crowded around them.

"*Squirrels!*" Mr. Pigeon grumbled as they alit. "A pox on them. Why doesn't the mayor do something about them?"

"I expect he's busy doing something else," said

Mrs. Pigeon. "Besides, they have as much right to the park as—"

But Mr. Pigeon had left her. He walked up to the nearest squirrel and pecked his tail. The squirrel dropped his peanut, jerked the attacked tail several times and said, "Say, who do you think you are?"

"Monitor of the head of William Tecumseh Sherman, general of Mr. Lincoln's army, overlord of the Plaza at Fifty-ninth Street," said Mr. Pigeon. He fixed the squirrel with a proud, ferocious eye. "And you?" His sneer expected nothing notable.

The squirrel squirmed. "Squirrel, ordinary grade, of the Children's Zoo," he said sheepishly. It certainly didn't sound impressive.

"I thought as much," said Mr. Pigeon. "Well, count yourself fortunate I don't run you off the place. Just keep your distance until I've dined."

"Yes, sir," said the squirrel, and he retired, looking surprised.

Mrs. Pigeon stared at her husband in wonder. How did he get away with it? He couldn't run a sparrow off a grating, let alone a squirrel out of the park, but when he took that tone other creatures just backed away. Even the speckled rowdy from Sixty-second Street had been awed until he decided to deal with Mr. Pigeon exactly as Mr. Pigeon had dealt with him. One day the speckled bird had blustered longer and louder than Mr. Pigeon, and when the storm was over the speckled bird was on the General's head and Mr. Pigeon was on the sidewalk.

What a silly world, Mrs. Pigeon thought, when words carry the day only if they're loud enough. She wondered whether this was true everywhere. New York City was the only world she knew, but migrating birds from time to time told her of other lands and places.

A mallard duck, stopping overnight on the Fifty-ninth Street lagoon, had once told her that there were places where one found no sidewalks, no lampposts, no buildings, no people, no pigeons.

"No pigeons?" Mrs. Pigeon had said suspiciously. "There are pigeons all over the world. Rome, Paris, Venice . . . pigeons everywhere. I happen to know that."

"Only where there are cities," the mallard duck

corrected. "There are vast areas of earth quite without a sign of cities."

Mrs. Pigeon's mind refused to accept this. What was there, if no city?

"Land and sea and sky. Desert. Plains and mountains," said the mallard duck, and Mrs. Pigeon shivered.

Now she watched Mr. Pigeon, that most citified of birds, advance upon his chosen person—a man with a beard and a bag of peanuts. Ruffling his feathers, muttering menacing coos, flashing his eyes, he scattered less confident birds to each side and then brashly, bravely, leaped to the bench beside the man, onto the very hand holding out peanuts.

Mrs. Pigeon, all admiration, picked up some nuts that her husband spilled down to her. He was a bold fellow, all right, and she was proud of him. But he apparently hadn't learned much from being shoved off General Sherman's head.

"Oh, deary me," she said to herself. "Deary me."

Suddenly the squirrel, who had been sitting on the

stone wall nursing his bruised tail and doing some
thinking, sat upright, paws folded against his chest,
nose quivering, tail jerking. He looked at Mr. Pigeon
with enormous indignation, dropped to his feet, sped
forward a little way, sat up again and chattered, "Say,
just who do you think you are, talking to me that
way?"

Mr. Pigeon glanced around loftily. "I told you. I sit on the head of General William Tec—"

Mrs. Pigeon looked away, embarrassed. Poor Mr. Pigeon. He couldn't admit the truth, even when the truth was not shameful at all but only a part of life. After all, had not he, in his day, forced a proud purple pigeon off the General's head?

"I don't care," the squirrel was saying, stretched out long now, almost at the side of the man, "I don't care if you lead General Sherman around by the nose, you can't talk to me that way."

"Come, my dear," said Mr. Pigeon to his wife. "We will go. I cannot remain in the society of people who show disrespect for our national heroes." With a drumming of wings, he set off for the Mall.

Mrs. Pigeon followed, thinking that it was not so much disrespect for General Sherman that the squirrel had shown as disrespect for Mr. Pigeon, who didn't even know it. He was not a bird to learn a lesson from rebuffs. She did not like to admit it, but she feared that Mr. Pigeon had no humility, no understanding that in Nature's great eye he was equal to, not above, other creatures.

"Oh, deary me," she said again, and fluttered in his wake.

They stopped briefly at the statue of Christopher Columbus, patron of pigeons. (Mr. Pigeon, who knew all sorts of facts, had told Mrs. Pigeon that *columba* is Latin for pigeon, and she had been very pleased to learn this.) Weathered and noble, Columbus looked, standing on his stone base, staring across at William Shakespeare on his marble one. Sun, rain, snow, sleet. Dawn, day, dark. Through it all stand the statues of Central Park, growing green and streaked with the years, not always noticed by people, but always, in all weather, loved by pigeons.

Mr. and Mrs. Pigeon stopped and thrust their round heads back and forth in a bobbing courtesy to this chief of pigeons, Christopher Columbus. Then they went on their way to a point across from the Goldman bandshell, where Mrs. Pigeon took her place on Victor Herbert and Mr. Pigeon fluttered a bit farther to roost

Columbus

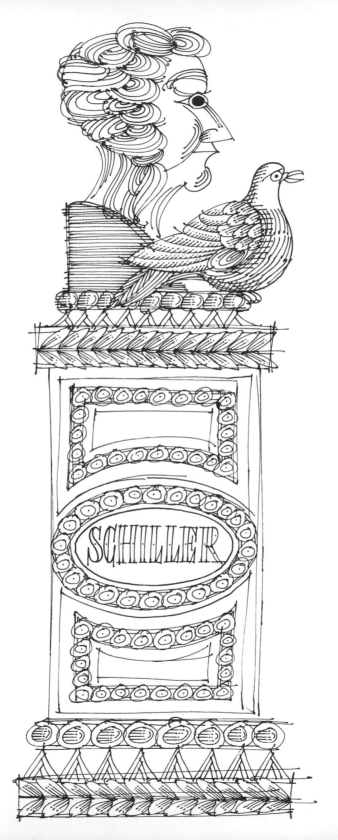

upon the shoulder of the poet Johann Christoph
Friedrich von Schiller.

Happily attempting to make a cadenza of a croomb,
Mrs. Pigeon was unaware of time passing. She started
when Mr. Pigeon, in a tremendous flap, landed beside
her and cried out, "I've got it!"

"Got what?" she gasped, looking him over to see
if anything was attached to him that shouldn't be.
Would she ever forget the time that bit of orange
wool got tangled around her foot? Why, it—

"I know now what is wrong with me," said Mr.
Pigeon in a voice of triumph.

"You mean why you're so cranky?"

"I am not cranky," he said crossly. "I am thought-
ful, perplexed and puzzled. But I am not cranky."

"Oh. Oh, well, then, that's all right," said Mrs.
Pigeon with relief. "All this time I thought you were."

"Well, I wasn't," he grumbled. "Do you or do you
not wish to hear what I have to say?"

"By all means."

"I'm tired of the city."

Mrs. Pigeon, who had begun to hum again, realized that she could not have heard correctly. "Just say that again, dear," she asked.

"I'm tired of the city."

"Tired of the city," Mrs. Pigeon repeated, to see if saying the words would make them more sensible. It seemed to make them less so. Tired of the *city?* *Tired* of the city? A fish might as well say he was tired of the water. "What do you mean, you're tired of the city?" she asked him. "What does that mean?"

"It means just what it says."

"But you can't be. You've lived here all your life."

"That's a good reason to be tired of it."

"But—but—but—"

"I want to retire."

"You already have," she said without thinking.

"I do not mean from William Tecumseh Sherman," he said coldly. "I wish to retire from the rigors of city living. From—" he said, ruffling suddenly "—the sight of hooligans like that!"

As he spoke, a gang of shrieking, quarreling star-

lings flashed into view, scattering sparrows and squirrels and even pigeons before their numerous, boister-
ous ranks. They tumbled and laughed and scolded.
The air rang with their shouts and quivered with their
darting, shining bodies.

"Hoodlums! Ruffians!" said Mr. Pigeon, getting up
on Victor Herbert's head. "Low fellows! They ought
to be forbidden the use of the park. They ought to
be run out of the city!"

Mrs. Pigeon said nothing. She knew that gangs of anything (except pigeons) made Mr. Pigeon nervous. And starlings did travel in gangs. Still, it seemed to her they had a right to the park, the same as jays or squirrels or people. Or pigeons, for that matter.

She watched the starlings, finding them quite dashing and gay, and wondered what Mr. Pigeon proposed to do now. How could he retire any more than he had already? They never saw anyone. They never went anywhere until driven by hunger.

How could he retire more?

All at once she had an inspiration. "We could fly down to Battery Park," she said brightly. "I have cousins there. Oh, that will be the very thing. We can ride on the Staten Island ferry, and see Wall Street and Trinity Church. I've always wanted to see Trinity Church."

"One does not retire to Battery Park," Mr. Pigeon said impatiently. "And your cousins are one of the things I want to get away from. Also sidewalks and automobiles and lampposts and fire alarms and squir-

24

rels and buses and starlings and all these buildings. I long for the free air, and the earth beneath my toes, and the wind in my wings."

"Deary me," said Mrs. Pigeon. "Perhaps we'd better go home and think some more."

They flew back to their ledge on the Plaza, and Mr. Pigeon stared across the park and Mrs. Pigeon stared at Mr. Pigeon staring.

The next morning a person in the hotel leaned out the window and waved his arms, shouting, "Shoo, shoo, you blasted pigeons! Shoo on out of here!"

"This is the last straw!" cried Mr. Pigeon as he tumbled off the ledge. When they'd found their wings and were flying along side by side, he said, "And *people*. I want to retire from people. My dear, are you coming with me?"

"Where, Mr. Pigeon?"

"I do not know. Away. Far away."

"Right now? You want to start now?"

"I," said Mr. Pigeon, wings moving powerfully, head stretched forward, "have already started. You are welcome to come along."

So Mrs. Pigeon assembled herself, changed from a flutter to a steady beat and followed her mate into retirement.

They flew very fast, as pigeons can but do not always bother to do, and presently they were speeding over Connecticut. Mrs. Pigeon slowed a bit and looked around, forcing Mr. Pigeon to do likewise.

"There's a pretty little park down there," she said. "It has a statue. Why don't we retire hereabouts? We

could go into the city every day and still have the advantages of country living."

Mr. Pigeon speeded up. "I will not become a commuter at my time of life," he told her and sped away. Mrs. Pigeon tore after him.

On they flew, and on and on.

About mid-Rhode Island, Mrs. Pigeon said, "Mr.

Pigeon, there is a Howard Johnson's down there. I am going to stop for a bite."

"Oh, very well," he agreed, being hungry himself by now.

They fluttered down past the orange and green roof to the parking lot, where they found a nearly full box of Cracker Jacks spilled under an Oldsmobile. They were fond of Cracker Jacks and dined well.

Then off again and on till dusk, when they were presented with a problem. Mr. and Mrs. Pigeon could roost in a tree, but preferred not to. A barn roof or a wooden fence did not suit them much better. What they wanted was a stone ledge.

What I want, Mrs. Pigeon moaned to herself, is the Plaza. But Mr. Pigeon was being brisk and cheery, allowing no doubts to cloud their trip into peaceful retirement. He led the way to an old weed-strewn graveyard and a flat stone marker smooth with the years.

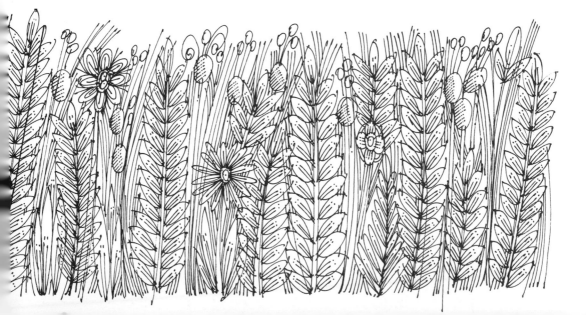

"There now," he said airily. "Isn't this ideal?"

Mrs. Pigeon looked around. "I wouldn't call it a home away from home," she said at last.

The sun, red as a traffic light, descended behind a ridge of dark mountains. It touched the treetops and the tilting markers in the graveyard with a warm flush. Around them were the sounds of birds going to nest.

All of them, Mrs. Pigeon noted, singers. This depressed her further. In the city, among the sparrows, starlings, jays and occasional seagulls, she could usually forget the passing song sparrow, the migrant thrush. But here—every thicket and field and tree seemed alive with beautiful voices. And not one of them hers.

She lifted her head high and willed with all her being one glorious clear note to issue forth and blend like a bell in the chorus around her. Just one note, she thought, equal to theirs, and I should be content. Pearly breast swelling, little beak parted, she sent forth her offering—

"*Croomb,*" it came, like a small, fat bubble. "Croomb, croomb, croomb." Like pebbles falling in a sidewalk puddle. *"Croomb."* Like—like a pigeon, she decided sadly.

Mr. Pigeon nudged her. "Look at all the beauty," he said. "Now, just take a look at all this beauty, will you?"

They looked. There was not a sidewalk, not a lamp-post, not a building to be seen. Only the trees and the fields and the humped hills. They looked at the sky wheeling above them. It was dark now, and stippled

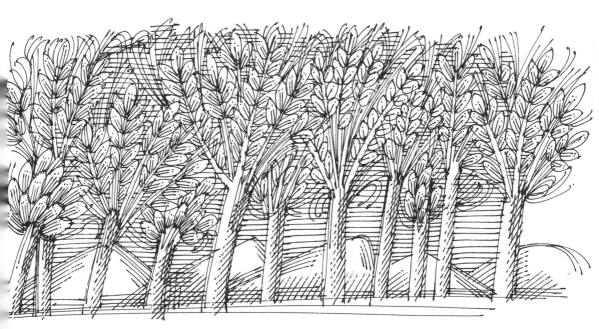

with stars. They felt the emptiness, the stillness, the vastness. This, thought Mrs. Pigeon, was what the mallard duck was talking about.

Then, as if so much beauty were too much beauty, she put her head under her wing and stopped looking.

In the morning Mr. Pigeon awakened and gazed about with a sinking heart. He was dismayed to find it all as big and as lonely as it had seemed the night before. To one side of them the rippling land stretched far away to the mountains. Ahead a dense forest rose like a warning. To the east he fancied he saw the glint of water.

This cheered him. Water meant rowboats, and rowboats meant people, and people meant food—beautiful lacy fragments of popcorn, heavy satisfying crusts of bread, warm rich peanuts.

In the prospect of food he revived more and more. How those roughnecks, those squirrels and starlings, would squirm to see him now—an adventurer like Christopher Columbus himself, and bolder than any of those puny city dwellers.

32

"Ah, how splendid," he said to his wife. He stretched up high, flapped his wings, tucked them neatly against his sides and strutted up and down the tombstone, flashing ecstatic glances from side to side.

Mrs. Pigeon, still as a bottle, slumped and stared, as he had on the Plaza ledge.

Mr. Pigeon looked at her anxiously. "It is a glorious morning," he said loudly. "Let us rejoice!"

"All right," she said, not moving.

He prodded her with his beak. "Up, up, my dear! Rejoice . . . rejoice!"

"I *am* rejoicing," she said nervously. "Just don't push."

Mr. Pigeon retreated a bit, preened his breast feathers and said with determination, "Yonder lies a body of water. Let us seek our breakfast there. I see in my mind's eye bursting bags of peanuts and pop—"

"That isn't the Seventy-ninth Street lake," she reminded him. "It's the Atlantic Ocean and the rocky coast of New England." Because of her good relationship with migratory birds, Mrs. Pigeon was quite strong on geography. "I don't believe we are apt—"

But Mr. Pigeon had already charged on, and resignedly Mrs. Pigeon took out after him.

For a long time after arriving at the ocean they said nothing. They sat uncomfortably on a jagged ledge of rock and looked. This time Mr. Pigeon did not comment upon the beauty.

Before them the waters stretched away, rolling and sliding, glittering in the sun. Behind them a black forest gave way to empty fields. To each side were cliffs and narrow stretches of rocky beach.

High in the sky swung the seagulls and cormorants and herons who made their home in this wilderness. Now and then a near-flying gull would look with surprise and superiority at the two rumpled pigeons and then angle off without a word.

"Just let me get them on the Mall," said Mr. Pigeon with a return of spirit. "I'd show them."

Mrs. Pigeon picked at a tangle of seaweed, found it inedible, tried a bit of fish dropped by some marauder and backed away.

At this very moment, she thought, her friends and relations down by the Pulitzer Fountain were exchanging the news of the day. In the zoo people would be strolling past the cages, spilling popcorn as they went. Right now, while she and Mr. Pigeon were being snubbed by seagulls, Schiller and Victor Herbert were listening to the cooing of other voices. At the Seventy-ninth Street lake people had tied up their rowboats to picnic on the grass, allowing birds and

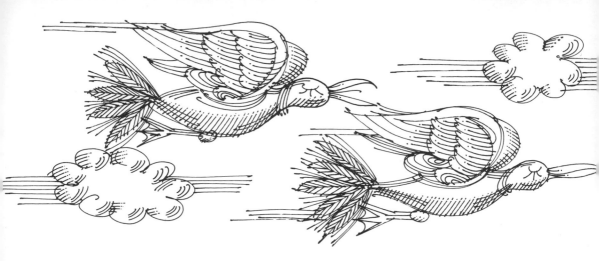

beasts to picnic on their crumbs. It was all so friendly,
so noisy, it was so wonderfully crowded, back there.

But here—oh, here were she and Mr. Pigeon, alone,
hungry, unbefriended.

She gazed at her mate as he stared at the passing cormorants and herons and gulls. They paid him no more
heed than if he had been a feather blown against the
cliff.

"Well, well, well," he said after a long time. "This
is more like it, eh? These fellows know how to keep
their place. Not like those—" He thought of the squirrels and starlings who, impudent though they might
be, certainly never ignored him. His voice trailed off
briefly, picked up again.

36

"My dear," he said, "we are now at the heart of Nature. It is a most welcome change, is it not, to be away from buildings and the clamor of traffic and the rowdy element in the park?"

"Croomb," said Mrs. Pigeon.

She wondered if she would ever in her life again see a strip of cement, a lamppost, a skylarking band of starlings or a plume-tailed squirrel. She wondered if she would ever find herself once again bowing along in the wake of a small boy with a balloon in one hand and a box of Cracker Jacks in the other.

Suddenly a great gray gull swept toward them through space. He landed a few feet away, wings held high and bent in fighting fashion.

"Who do you think you are?" he boomed. "Get away from my rock!"

Mrs. Pigeon got behind Mr. Pigeon, who quailed a moment but then said steadily enough, "I am Pigeon, monitor of the head of General William Tecumseh Sherman, at your service, sir."

"I never heard of him or you," said the gull. "On your way, both of you, before I run you off."

"Now, see here," Mr. Pigeon began, but the advancing seagull loomed so large that he changed his mind and said hurriedly to Mrs. Pigeon, "Fly. I will follow when you've got started." He said loudly, "This rock, my dear, is not only ugly, it is inhabited by brigands. Let us find pleasanter surroundings."

The two pigeons took off in a fast flutter.

"Imagine," Mr. Pigeon grumbled later when they were exploring a field—some distance from the ocean —where they hoped to find wind-blown grain. "Imagine talking that way to a tourist. Fellow has no manners at all."

"I thought his manners seemed very familiar," Mrs.

38

Pigeon said tartly, but to that her husband made no answer.

So the peaceful retirement began.

Each night, on the flat stone marker in the little graveyard, they huddled with their heads under their wings. Each day they ranged the wild fields and forests in search of berries and nuts and grain. They grew thin. Mrs. Pigeon noticed that she had no desire any more to hum, much less attempt song. She thought it was for lack of Victor Herbert. She also observed that she and Mr. Pigeon talked less and less. Maybe pigeons, she thought, are meant to be together, in a chorus, cooing.

What's wrong with cooing? she asked herself suddenly. She recalled the stirring band of her fellows all over the streets and rooftops and spires of New York. What could be more harmonious than that honey-thick purling of notes, the concert of the pigeons? Some birds were meant to sing solo arias. Some were meant to swell the chorus. Was one more honorable, more necessary, than the other? No, no, she said to her-

self, aquiver with the longing to be, once again, part of that giant chant on the sidewalks of New York.

But Mr. Pigeon stubbornly pointed out the beauties of retirement. He could not admit, to her or to himself, that his great and daring move had been a mistake.

The days grew shorter and the nights longer. The wind began to show its teeth. More than once Mr. and Mrs. Pigeon were taken and shaken like little flags in a tornado. They abandoned the open fields and stayed close to the forest, where the trees were some

protection. Sometimes Mrs. Pigeon would look at the towering trunks, the wildly waving branches, and pretend that these were Central Park trees, just grown a bit thicker and taller. But each time she ventured right into the woods the illusion vanished. The tree trunks soared into a wilderness of sky and tossing branches, and a feeling of smallness would overcome her. She'd flap her way quickly to the field again and, side by side with Mr. Pigeon, peck about in search of food.

Meanwhile Mr. Pigeon went nervously from stumps to boulders to gravestones, trying to find something he could use as a statue. But nothing looked or felt like General Sherman, or Schiller, or Christopher Columbus.

Finally, one stormy morning, he said to himself, Perhaps I was wrong. I had my time of greatness on the General's head, but it is the way of the world that one pigeon should replace another pigeon, as—no doubt—one general replaces another general.

"Perhaps I was wrong!" he said, out loud this time.

But the wind carried his voice away, and, besides, he was all alone.

Just then a brilliant form flashed toward him through the sky and landed with a whistle at his side. It was the mallard duck who in spring and fall stopped on the Fifty-ninth Street lagoon.

"I said to myself," the duck told Mr. Pigeon. "I *said* to myself as I passed the edge of the woods over there, surely that is Mrs. Pigeon, whose absence all the pigeons of the park are bemoaning? Then I spied you and said to myself, and there is *Mr.* Pigeon, prominent past president of General Sherman's head. And, you see, I was quite right," he congratulated himself.

"My eyesight certainly isn't going back on me, is it, now?"

"No," said Mr. Pigeon, more joyful than he cared to admit at this news from home. "No, it has not, sir. How very good to see you again. On your way north, I presume?"

"Yes, yes. I'm to rejoin the flock in Nova Scotia. Stopped off to see a cousin of mine in Sudbury, Massachusetts. Do you know Sudbury?"

"No," said Mr. Pigeon. "No, the fact is, Mrs. Pigeon and I came directly here." He did not add that he still wasn't at all sure where here was.

"Fine little town," said the duck.

"Town?" said Mr. Pigeon, looking around.

"Sudbury," said the duck a bit impatiently. "Where my cousin lives. He was a wild duck, mind you, but took up with this family of people when his wing was injured in a storm last year. He's never left them. I stopped to see him, find out if he wanted to come with us again. But he's become oddly attached to people."

"So am I," said Mr. Pigeon without thinking. Once

the words were out, he was struck by the truth in them. It was true. He missed not only the statues, the sidewalks, the church steeples and hotel ledges, not only the peanuts and popcorn and picnic crusts. He missed the people. He was used to them, going about on their busy legs, keeping the zoo animals company, playing chess in the sun, feeding pigeons, putting up statues for pigeons, being *there* for pigeons in such a reliable and unselfish manner. What if one did shoo him off a window ledge from time to time? With all their virtues, it now seemed a small offense.

He sighed, and the duck said, "When are you thinking of starting back?"

"Back?"

"You hardly plan to stay here all winter, old man? It isn't your habitat. You'll starve. Or freeze. Mark you, I think it was pretty daring, coming all the way up here just because you got in a huff—"

"I did not get in a huff," Mr. Pigeon huffed.

"You didn't?" The duck sounded surprised. "That's the way I heard it."

46

Mr. Pigeon's throat swelled indignantly. So that's what they were saying, was it? And he not there to defend himself, to explain that he—that he—

"We felt like going on a trip," he said loudly. "What's wrong with that?"

"Not a thing in the world, old boy. It's just that pigeons don't generally travel, you know. Homebodies, one might call you, in fact."

"Nonsense," said Mr. Pigeon. "How about that pigeon from the St. Regis who went to Naples last year?"

"An exception. Besides, he took a boat. Traveled on the *Cristoforo Colombo,* come to think of it. How appropriate. Anyway, it's warm in Italy. I imagine a pigeon could settle down in Naples or Venice or Rome and never know he'd left home. But to come up here! Well . . . that's bravery for you."

Mr. Pigeon looked modestly down at his pink toes, pleased by the duck's choice of words. Still, he could not put out of mind that "You'll freeze, you'll starve." And he could not dismiss the ruffling thought of those fellows flapping around the Pulitzer Fountain saying that he, Mr. Pigeon, couldn't take it, that he had run away in a huff.

"Ah," said the duck. "Here comes your good wife."

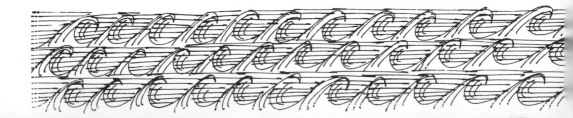

Mrs. Pigeon was joyous at the sight of this old friend from the lagoon. She settled beside him and they plunged into talk of "Do you remember, and how is this one and that one, and how was the lagoon looking when last you looked, and are the people skating yet at Wollman Rink—" All the things one would naturally ask at such a meeting.

Meanwhile Mr. Pigeon turned matters over in his mind. Perhaps the time had arrived for him to come out of retirement. Well-traveled pigeons, such as he and his wife, would be an adornment to any company, of that there could be no question. If they returned to New York, they would be the center of attention. For a while, he added, having learned that no one remains in the center. That seemed fair enough. To be the center of attention for a while would be gratifying. To be such all the time would no doubt prove boring to a pigeon like himself, who preferred to roost quietly on Schiller and think.

"What do you mean," he could hear himself say, "what do you mean, *ran away?* Can't a pigeon take a brief trip without all you gossips pouncing?" *That* would ruffle them. Nothing a gossip hated worse than being called a gossip. He would look at them scornfully, and at that point would chuckle to himself. "Ran away, *in*deed!" he'd chuckle. "That's rich." Then, dropping the real news—which would circulate quickly, depend upon it—he'd say, "Mrs. Pigeon and I thought a run up to—to the New England coast would be the very thing before I take up my new position on the Mall."

"New position?" they'd say, astounded, clucking and curious.

"Hadn't you heard?" he'd reply, surprised, but tolerant of their ignorance. "I'm appointed to the bust of Johann Christoph Friedrich von Schiller. I wish to say that General Sherman has been a fruitful, meaningful, heartwarming experience in my life, but I never intended to make the military a *career*. My own interests, as you know, lie with the arts—"

Ah, *yes*. His pearly breast swelled with emotion as he heard in fancy the respectful and admiring chorus of croombs from the foot of the fountain.

He was thinking about this, seeing the scene, hearing the sounds, when all at once his dreams of glory were invaded by a sudden sharp yearning for the city of New York. Especially, he realized with a catch in his throat, for the park at Fifty-ninth Street. In that moment he knew that if he never had charge of even a drinking fountain again, he wanted to go home. He'd patrol the General's horse's feet or the subway entrance on Fifth Avenue—just so he could be home again.

52

He looked about at the black forests, the rocky fields, the faraway metallic glint of the ocean, and knew that the mallard duck was right. He and Mrs. Pigeon did not have their habitat here. They were homebodies, and their home was the city.

And so in the vast and lonely face of Nature, Mr. Pigeon at last felt humble.

He and Mrs. Pigeon returned to the ledge on the Plaza. They became, as Mr. Pigeon had foreseen, the brief and noisy center of attention. But Mr. Pigeon did not boast of his travels. He did not claim an appointment to the shoulder of Schiller. One day he just quietly took up his station and was accepted by all as the poet's rightful guardian.

Starlings, squirrels, jays and sparrows brawled down the pathways, across the lawns of the Mall, and Mr. Pigeon watched them peacefully.

"In Nature's great eye," he murmured to Herr Schiller (who did not disagree), "we are all one."

"Now, I'm extremely glad to hear you say that," said the squirrel from the Children's Zoo, curving his plumy tail. "You certainly have changed since your trip."

"Travel alters one's perspective," Mr. Pigeon agreed.

"Do you plan another journey?" asked the squirrel.

Mr. Pigeon shivered. "Not immediately," he said. "Shall we go over to the chess arena and have a bite?"

"By all means, friend," said the squirrel, and off they went.